THE Christmas List

OTHER BOOKS BY ED J. PINEGAR

The Christmas Code

THE Christmas List

a novella by
Ed J. Pinegar

Covenant Communications, Inc.

Cover image: *Christmas Decoration* © sofiaworld, courtesy istockphoto.com.

Cover design copyright © 2016 by Covenant Communications, Inc.

Published by Covenant Communications, Inc.
American Fork, Utah

Copyright © 2016 by Ed J. Pinegar
All rights reserved. No part of this book may be reproduced in any format or in any medium without the written permission of the publisher, Covenant Communications, Inc., P.O. Box 416, American Fork, UT 84003. The views expressed within this work are the sole responsibility of the author and do not necessarily reflect the position of Covenant Communications, Inc., or any other entity.

This is a work of fiction. The characters, names, incidents, places, and dialogue are either products of the author's imagination, and are not to be construed as real, or are used fictitiously.

Printed in the United States of America
First Printing: October 2016

22 21 20 19 18 17 16   10 9 8 7 6 5 4 3 2 1

ISBN 978-1-68047-631-6

Acknowledgments

I express gratitude to my sweetheart, Pat, for her listening ear. Thanks to Emily Halverson, whose expert editing and magnificent ideas made everything better. To my Covenant friends, Kathy and Samantha, thank you for your editorial help. And most of all, I give thanks for the inspiration from above that brought this idea to my heart.

Preface

In *The Christmas Code*, the novella preceding this work, Mr. G, an elderly man filled with regret for past mistakes, looks forward to what may well be his final celebration of the birth of Christ in this life. A people-watcher, he attempts to assuage his guilt by sharing the Christian message of goodness and hope through number- and color-coded messages and simple acts of kindness with people he meets in his neighborhood. Unfortunately, his regret keeps him from enjoying for himself the peace this message should bring.

Just a few days before Christmas, his messages and acts of kindness create a chain reaction of positive effects in five people's lives, inspiring in them hope and the desire to make others happy. The resulting events come full circle for Mr. G, culminating in a poignant reunion and the resolution of his most painful regret, just before his death.

In *The Christmas List*, the characters from *The Christmas Code* live on with the inspiration of Mr. G and his journal. All have transcending moments in their lives through Mr. G's and his grandson, Jacob's, encouragement. Lives are touched and changed as each person seeks to find and live the true spirit of Christmas.

Prologue
A MESSAGE AND A CHALLENGE

Frozen sleet pelted against Jacob's bedroom window, driving him deeper into his navy flannel bedding. It was mid-December, and a frigid winter had come on fast. As the bitter wind howled through his backyard trees, Jacob struggled to relax and drift off to sleep. Even though he was no longer a little boy, violent storms like this one still made him uneasy.

After a few restless minutes, he sat up with a sigh of defeat, flicked on his bedside lamp, and grabbed a worn-looking notebook off his nightstand. Its familiar heft instantly soothed him—his grandfather's journal was one of the few links Jacob had to that great man, Matthew Good, or Mr. G, since he had passed, and he felt calmer and closer to him every time he opened it.

As he flipped through its pages, he came to something he'd never noticed before. Because the journal was not full, cut short by Mr. G's passing, Jacob never bothered flipping through the second half of the journal. But just now he discovered that in the midst of those empty final pages, there were several sheets stuck together. He tried to separate them, causing the bottom corner of one page to slightly rip. Quickly changing tactics, Jacob opened his end-table drawer and fished out his trusty Boy Scout pocketknife. He slid the thinnest blade between the pages and gently moved the knife around. Some of the edges tore a little, but he pressed on undeterred. As he carefully pulled the pages apart, he inhaled sharply with excitement.

The entire two pages were in code—a code he had long ago learned by heart. He deciphered the note with ease.

*10 Ways
to Recapture the Christmas Spirit:*

As Jacob read over the ten ideas, he was surprised by the list. Some of the items seemed to have little to do with Christmas itself. Then he noticed a note at the bottom of the page that Mr. G had scrawled out with seeming excitement:

Could doing each of these things really work to rekindle the magic of Christmas in people's lives? How I'd love to implement this experiment with others before I die . . .

As Jacob lay there with his grandfather's words in his hands, memories of that special holiday season ten years ago flooded his mind—Christmas Eve dinner with his grandpa and his dog, as well as their anonymous benefactor, and the magic and excitement of that special time of year. Although he was far from being cynical, Jacob realized with a twinge of guilt that he could use some Christmas rekindling himself.

He read on:

Wouldn't it be wonderful if this Christmas we would be a little friendlier and be grateful for all our blessings in life. If we could find happiness and spread cheer to everyone we see, maybe we could seek to understand and be encouraging to all. And wouldn't it be wonderful if pride was dispelled and we could be humble, kind, and gentle. We would see the hand of God in our lives and be forgiving and never hold a grudge, and then we could be good and full of charity and be like Jesus. To me, that's the essence—the magic—of the Christmas spirit. To be like Jesus! That is what matters.

December twenty-fifth was barely more than a week away. Did the holiday still incite that same wonder he'd felt as a little boy? Though only a teenager, Jacob wondered if he was already guilty of the very yuletide apathy his grandfather had lamented. But he couldn't go back to being a kid, listening in anticipation for Santa's heavy footsteps on the roof. Would following Grandpa's ten suggestions really work to recapture the Christmas spirit?

Jacob quickly glanced at his watch to check the date. "December fourteenth," he whispered to himself.

With pencil in hand, he excitedly made an inspired amendment to his grandpa's list.

*10 ~~Ways~~ DAYS
to Recapture the Christmas Spirit*

Chapter One
A FORGOTTEN FRIEND

"*Everyone?* Here in this little kitchen?" Maggie repeated doubtfully, tucking a stray curl behind her ear. She had been cleaning up some late-night dishes when Jacob had surprised her by bursting into the kitchen with his sudden idea. She thought he'd long been asleep. "Jacob, it's not necessarily a bad idea. I just wonder if we would all fit. And I'm not even sure if everyone still lives around here. I mean, we do exchange Christmas cards every year, and I guess no one has mentioned an address change . . ." Maggie trailed off uncertainly, then smiled gently at her son.

Just then a clap of lightning lit the bay window behind Maggie, and she startled a bit.

Jacob went on undeterred. "Please, Mom. It would be so great to see everyone again . . . and have us all *together* for the holidays in honor of Grandpa. I can see the byline on our invitation: Mr. G's Legacy Lives On."

"To honor Grandpa? Out of the blue? Your standard dinner-between-Thanksgiving-and-Christmas party?" she teased.

"And why not?" Jacob shot back playfully. "Look, Mom. I can't tell you all the reasons I have up my sleeve because it would ruin the surprise. The main thing is I just think it would be fun to see everyone—Mrs. White, Jeremy and his new wife, the Thompsons—everyone! I mean, Christmastime is when we all first met over ten years ago. And I think it's about time we all reunited! Don't you think Grandpa would want that?" Jacob asked, flashing Maggie his disarming grin.

* * *

Maggie gazed at her handsome son and wondered where her little boy had gone. He was sixteen now and gifted in so many ways. His own journal reflected writing skills beyond his years. And he had always been a people lover. Maggie admired his enthusiasm for others and for life itself. It wasn't exactly that she was antisocial; it was just that she had almost completely let go of that side of life—or perhaps more specifically, she had given up hope.

The Christmas List 7

Instead, for the past decade, she'd thrown herself into raising her boy, making sure he had all his emotional needs tended to, and she had just ignored her own. *And that's what will make me the happiest*, she told herself. Although in her more lonely and honest moments, she couldn't help but hope that God had more in mind for her.

"Mom, believe me; it won't be too hard to gather everyone. You see Chase and Alexa at work every day, so inviting them and Matthew Jr. will be a cinch. And I know where Grandpa's old building is. It would be easy for me to just walk over there and knock on Mrs. White's and Jeremy's doors."

"That's true," Maggie admitted.

"Oh, Mom, it's going to be so great. We'll share stories we remember about Grandpa and what we've been doing since he brought us all together."

"Well, it actually might be fun to make a big holiday dinner. Haven't done that in a while." Maggie walked to the corner of the room and opened her antique hutch, murmuring more to herself than anyone else, "I wonder where all my holiday china is?" She absentmindedly began humming the first few bars of "Good Christian Men, Rejoice!"

"Don't worry, Mom. You'll invite the Thompsons and make sure they bring Matthew Jr., and I'll invite everyone from the apartments."

"But tomorrow night?" Maggie squeaked. "Why so soon? Jacob, no one is going to be able to come on this short notice!"

"Why not? I mean, it's worth a shot. Tomorrow is Saturday, so it's as good a chance as any." Jacob imitated his mom's hands-on-hips stance, and she could tell he was determined. "It will work. It just has to. I have a good feeling about it. You will understand the urgency better tomorrow at our get-together." Jacob gave her a charming wink and then charged on before she could object. "So I was thinking that Mr. Thompson is often at the office on Saturday mornings, right? You could drop by there first and invite his family. I will go by the apartments in the morning too, and that will still give me enough time to pick up what you what me to buy for party food before I get home. It's going to be great!" Jacob leaned over, pecked his mom on the cheek, and ran up the stairs to his bedroom before she could get a word in edgewise.

* * *

Once upstairs, Jacob flopped onto his bed with a peaceful sigh and reached for his grandpa's journal again. *Mom's going to love this*, he thought to himself. She just needed a little help, a little social motivation in the right direction. He reread his grandpa's ten-item list and felt a jolt of excitement course through him. "I'm actually going to give the entire group a little bit of help. By the end of tomorrow night, they will have *all* fulfilled step number one," he whispered to himself. Looking at his grandpa's first invitation, he couldn't help but grin.

Seek out a forgotten friend

* * *

Maggie's dining room was abuzz with excitement. As Jeremy's wife, Jeanie, took in the festively decorated dinner table and all the happy chatter, she couldn't help but feel a little out of place. Of course everyone had been very kind and inviting, but it seemed like they all shared such a strong connection. And they all appeared so . . . well, happy.

A light animated all the faces around her—a light she was certain was absent from her own. *Although, if they'd gone through what I have this past year . . .* she thought to herself. She pushed the fresh memory of her mother's cancer-ravaged body out of her mind. Watching her mom's steely-gray casket lowered into the ground was one of the sharpest agonies she had ever felt. *Never mind all the prayers I said. And to think I believed someone was actually listening.*

Alexa Thompson's inquiry brought Jeanie's thoughts back to the present. "So, Jeanie, remind me how long you and Jeremy have been married."

"Let's see. I guess almost three years now. We met in a G.E. biology class at the community college, and the rest is history," Jeanie responded, forcing a smile.

"Well, glad to see your education wisened you up sufficiently, Jeremy," Alexa's husband,

Chase, quipped. "You'd have been a fool to let this one go!" Chase smiled at Jeanie warmly.

"You aren't kidding!" Jeremy agreed. "If it weren't for Mrs. White's encouragement to go back to school, it wouldn't just be my degree I'd have missed out on."

"Remind me what you studied in school," Maggie said, getting up from the table to refill the water pitcher.

"Construction management, actually, with a minor in business," Jeremy said. "Helping Mrs. White manage her apartment building over the years showed me how much I enjoyed the business aspect of things. And it worked out great to keep that job while getting through school. The practical application of all I was learning in my classes really helped."

"Not to mention the added bonus that this kept him close to me all these years," Mrs. White said. "I'm getting up there in years, you know. Jeremy has been just like a dear son to me, watching out for me. And watching him bloom has been my greatest joy. And Jeanie? Well, she has only added to our family." Mrs. White paused, resting her gaze on the young married couple. "Yes, Mr. White would have been proud to pass his business to such a fine young man and his family. I couldn't ask for more. And to think this is all thanks to Mr. G." Her eyes glistened.

"Here, here!" several of them echoed heartily in agreement, nodding their heads.

"Speaking of which," Jacob interjected, standing up from the table to unfold his long, lanky frame. "I have an announcement to make. But first I want to thank you all for coming here on such short notice. My saintly mother was so kind to accommodate my wild but wonderful idea from my grandpa, whom we all love. I assure you—"

"No need to convince us, Jacob," Alexa said, reaching over to dish up fourteen-year-old Matthew Jr. seconds of Maggie's buttery mashed potatoes. "Tonight has been a delight."

"Well, it's about to get even better," Jacob said with an infectious mixture of mystery and excitement. "How would each of you like to receive one final coded message from my grandpa? A message to top all messages, which could potentially affect your life more than any of his previous ones did."

Maggie stirred in her seat, looking uncomfortable, seeming to not know what her son was suggesting. "What could you possibly mean, Jake? Are you joking?"

"I've never been more serious. A special *Christmas* message, no less. From your dad straight to us on this very evening."

All eyes were fastened on Jacob, and from the looks on everyone's faces, he could tell he could prolong the suspense no longer. "Last night I discovered a coded message at the end of Grandpa's journal. It was a list, a list of challenges he seemed to want those closest to him to put to the test. Basically his dying wish."

"What kind of challenges?" Chase asked anxiously.

"Even better than telling you, I'll *read* it to you." Jacob sat back down and reached under his seat for the book he'd carefully concealed before everyone had arrived. Flipping to the journal's final pages, he explained, "Now, before we get to the list, listen to what Grandpa wrote *after* listing the ten things he wanted us to do."

He cleared this throat and read his grandpa's statement: "Could doing each of these things really work to rekindle the magic of Christmas in people's lives? How I'd love to try out this experiment with others before I die . . ."

"Wow," Maggie said. "What a treasure, son. What are the ten things Grandpa listed?"

"Well, before I tell you all, I want to first share with you a thought I had soon after reading this list. And I can't help but feel that Grandpa inspired it." Jacob paused, his gaze resting on each eager face. "How many of you are up for trying out this challenge? Grandpa's dying wish. Ten things he was sure would rekindle the magic of Christmas in their lives. The timing is perfect because we have exactly ten days until Christmas. Each day we will accomplish a task until the ten days are complete. And I already helped you with the first one," he said with a wink.

"Really?" Mrs. White said. "So what does the list contain, dear boy? Do tell! And how on earth could we have already accomplished number one?"

"You accomplished it when you all so willingly agreed to reunite here tonight on such short notice. I told you it'd be worth it."

"Well, I, for one, can say I am totally game for this challenge . . . before I even need to hear what's on the list. If Mr. G created it, that's all I need to know," Chase said excitedly. He stood carefully from the table, then moved away and started pacing around the dining room. "But do read on, Jacob. What are the ten things?"

"So we're all in?" Jacob asked. "We have completed step one tonight, and there are ten days left until Christmas, which means we will complete the final challenge on Christmas Eve."

All heads nodded eagerly except for one. Jeanie didn't disagree aloud; she just felt she should refrain from saying anything until she learned more. For some reason, she'd felt instantly reluctant. Perhaps she doubted somewhere inside that any list—no matter how wise its content—could bring her Christmas joy this season. Or any season to come for that matter.

"I think it would be more exciting if I revealed each new step to you one day at a time. I promise you there is no step Grandpa suggested that cannot be accomplished within each appointed day. I've already created a blog we can use as our communication forum. I was thinking that each morning I could post Grandpa's new challenge for the day. And every evening we can all report back and post comments about how our day went while putting to the test what Grandpa envisioned. What do you think?"

"But you haven't even told us what step number one is," Jeremy said, laughing.

"Oh yeah!" Jacob said. "How could I forget? Step number one is simply this: seek out a forgotten friend." He grinned. "And thanks to my mom's incredible meal—and even more impressive, her willingness to go along with my hair-brained ideas—I hope we can all agree that tonight has served that purpose."

All heads bobbed up and down in agreement. Even Jeanie's, although she was sure Mr. G's ideas could not melt her frozen heart no matter how inspired they all claimed him to be.

"So what is the address for the blog?" Alexa asked. "I'm dying to see it."

"I thought you'd never ask!" Jacob joked. He looked around happily and said simply, as if there could be no other alternative, "MrGsLegacyLivesOn.blogspot.com."

Chapter Two
GRATITUDE TO ALL

Forcing her way through a sleepy haze, Maggie sat up in bed and silenced her chipper alarm clock. Even though she'd just awoken, an unexpected hope filled her heart. She strained to remember any dream she'd had overnight in an effort to understand the source of the hope.

And then it hit her. *The list Jacob found! It's like I'm able to converse with my dad again.*

Jumping out of bed, Maggie hurried over to her closet to fish out her dad's royal blue robe—the one she'd found and kept after his passing. Its satiny fabric smelled of spicy aftershave, and putting it on always made her feel a little closer to him.

Although it was still early, she booted up her laptop in hopeful anticipation. After finding the blog's website that Jacob had told them about, she gasped in excitement as she read the blog's title in festive green letters across the top of the page.

Ten Ways to Recapture the Christmas Spirit:
Mr. G's Legacy Lives On

Hungrily she read on and discovered that Jacob had been up late last night creating the blog's very first post.

December 15
Challenge #1—Be a friend: seek out a forgotten friend

Congratulations, everyone! Without even breaking a sweat, tonight you fulfilled challenge #1! ☺ Hope everyone found it as fun as I did.

My discussion question for this opening challenge is simple: how can reconnecting with forgotten friends open your heart more to the Christmas spirit? What might Grandpa have had in mind?

Post your thoughts below—and good luck tomorrow with challenge #2!

~Jacob

Maggie was shocked to see there was already a comment posted. Not only that, but Jacob had been up much earlier than she that morning and had posted the day's challenge. She hesitated a moment, deciding whether to read on and find out challenge #2 or pause here and contribute. She decided to pace herself and linger on the challenge #1 post a bit longer. She would savor every bite of this candy bar for as long as she could.

Unsurprised, she discovered the first post was from Mr. Go-Get-'Em, Chase Thompson. What did surprise her was his tone. Her usually carefree and optimistic employer seemed to write with a preoccupied heaviness she'd never known in him.

2:32 a.m.—Comment #1

From Chase: Couldn't sleep so I decided to get up to see if this blog had gone live yet. Glad to see the first post and challenge are already up.

You ask a great question, Jacob. Speaking for myself, I know it's easy in life to get caught up in the thick of thin things. And then suddenly something happens that completely alters your superficial paradigm—be it a conversation, an experience, even a tragedy.

Being with old friends, those who know me, reminds me of who I really am. It has the ability to cut through mortality's mundane fog and reach me with heavenly reminders of my divine identity and worth. You know the old saying that a friend is someone "who knows your song and will sing it back to you when you've forgotten the tune"? Something like that.

Seeing all of you tonight "sang back to me my tune," in a way. No matter how hard life can be, how difficult the things we are called on to face, if we are surrounded by those we love and filled with an awareness of our own divine potential, we can face our trials with strength. This awakening to who we really are can only open our hearts more to who our Savior is. And thus the true spirit of Christmas can enter.

At least that was my experience. Excited to hear from all of you . . .

Maggie sat for a while and digested Chase's post. While his sober pensiveness was uncharacteristic, his words were nevertheless true, and they struck a chord deep in her heart. Connecting with those you love and who love you in return really did remind her of who she was. And with no one was that more true than with her father. Ever since that Christmas years ago when she had met him, she had never seen herself the same. Or the saving ability of her Savior. Maggie pulled her father's robe closer around her and felt enveloped in the arms of his love. She knew she was his little girl and there was something waiting for her. Something special.

* * *

Riding the train to her work downtown, Jeanie pulled out her tablet to pass the time. *What was the blog address Jacob mentioned last night? Something about Mr. G never dying . . .* She racked her brain, then shot her husband a quick text to see if he remembered.

She didn't have to wait more than a few seconds for Jeremy's reply. *MrGsLegacyLivesOn.blogspot.com*

That's right. She sighed to herself, the same reluctance returning. *Well, let's take a look, shall we? Even though I've accomplished his first challenge and feel no different, the least I can do is read the suggestions the man gives—this person who practically saved my husband's life. I at least owe him that.*

Chase's post alarmed her. Did he really know as much about facing difficult things as he was currently implying? With his successful law firm, his loving wife and son . . . Jeanie had just been with him last night, and he had been all smiles. She found it hard to see how life could be challenging him at the moment.

Her attention moved on to the second post.

December 16
Challenge #2—Be grateful: express gratitude and thanksgiving to all

Hello, everyone! Are you ready for this? Day two, and it's going to be a good one!

Don't forget to check back in tonight and leave us a quick post about how your day went. Especially the connections you make between expressing gratitude and the Christmas spirit. Good luck!

Anxiously waiting,
~Jacob

As Jeanie finished reading challenge #2, she felt her body relax a bit. *Expressing gratitude—that's easy enough.* She was relieved it wouldn't force her out of her comfort zone as far as she feared some of these challenges might.

She felt eager to check off the boxes Mr. G was providing, if only to prove to what she

The Christmas List   23

already knew about herself. As she stood to get off the train, she thanked the man in front of her for letting her exit first, then the woman coming out of the train station for picking up her purse after it dropped. After the short walk from the train, Jeanie sailed through her workplace door, singing out a "Thank you" to the security guard who let her in.

She strode through the office to her cubicle in the back, then sank down into her chair. "That was three thank yous in a row," she whispered to herself. "Do I feel any different?"

She looked around the office at the garland her boss had strung from cubicle to cubicle, then at the tinsel Happy Holidays sign hanging over the entrance. Numbly she threw her frozen heart into the work ahead of her—disappointed but not surprised.

* * *

Challenge #2—Be grateful: express gratitude to all you meet
8:45 p.m.—Comment #1

From Maggie: Well, I have to say, everyone—today really surprised me!

I mean, I see myself as a pretty grateful person. But, wow, do I have a long way to go! What a difference it made today, expressing thanks to everyone I could!! I started noticing things people do for me, all around me, that I had never before acknowledged.

The biggest difference this challenge made for me was recognizing all the little things one of my coworkers does for me. He's another admin assistant, Zach Jones, whom Chase and Alexa hired at the beginning of the year. It's like it was the first time I really noticed his presence in the office. He was constantly doing little things for me that I had been taking for granted—refilling my printer with paper, asking if I needed him to bring back lunch, even gathering my mail to send out at the end of the day. I kept saying small thank yous throughout the day, but this evening as we left the office, I looked him right in the eyes (for the first time) and said, "Zach, you really are a big help to me around the office. I want to thank you for that."

He looked kind of taken aback, then stammered, "Uh, well, I'm glad you noticed. And it's no big thing. You do so much for this entire office, I guess a few of us can afford to help you in return." What a kind thing to say, no?

I have definitely felt closer to the Savior through today's challenge. He was the master at noticing and thanking everyone around Him. It's made me remember the account of Jesus noticing Zacchaeus up in the tree. I've always loved how that story shows how aware the Savior is of all around Him. Hey, wait a minute . . . I wonder if Zach is short for Zacchaeus? Well, wouldn't that be interesting?! I'll have to ask him tomorrow. Funny, today's exercise has even made me look forward more to work. I feel good all over. Can expressing gratitude make such a difference in one day?

Thank you, Jacob, for this experience. And thank you, Daddy, for changing my life once again.

xoxo,

Maggie

Chapter Three
ASSUME THE GOOD

Alexa slowed her sprint into a light jog as she rounded the block and her Tudor-style home came into view. Glimmering yet fading stars were still visible in the early-dawn sky, although they would vanish in minutes as the horizon brightened into shades of lighter blue. Quietly slipping in through the back door, she lightly jogged up the stairs, careful not to wake her sleepy household. She fumbled in the darkness as she passed through her bedroom, pausing momentarily to notice Chase's peaceful form slumbering under their down comforter, his chest rising and falling with each breath. How she missed him accompanying her on these early-morning runs. It had been months since he had joined her. Work had been taking its toll on him, it seemed, and lately he had been opting to use that time in the morning for extra rest.

Stepping into a steamy hot shower, Alexa's thoughts remained on her husband as she went through her morning routine. She was grateful she had shopped for his Christmas present earlier in the year and would not have to scramble around last-minute, fighting all the holiday shoppers and crowds. *Grateful.* That had become a familiar feeling for Alexa over the past twenty-four hours, thanks to Mr. G's challenge. She was surprised how much a conscious effort to acknowledge her blessing had affected her outlook.

After she dressed for the day, she searched her bedroom closet for Chase's present. Luckily the small Swiss-army watch was not a hard gift to hide. Reaching behind a bin of stored summer clothes, she brushed her hand against something unfamiliar. She grabbed it and pulled out a sealed manila folder. Since they didn't usually store paperwork in their closet, Alexa slipped open the envelope to find what filing items might have become lost in the shuffle.

"That's strange," she whispered under her breath as she pulled out a small stack of paperwork. It appeared to be a collection of medical bills from the office of a Dr. Richard Stoltz.

The Christmas List 29

The doctor's name rang a bell, and Alexa quickly jogged her memory as to where she'd heard that name before. Ah yes, the podiatrist Chase had been seeing over the past few months due to some foot pain that had been giving him issues now and then. She recalled seeing Dr. Stoltz's name come up on their bank statements.

She absentmindedly flipped through the first few bills, wondering why they had been filed here rather than their home office. Then she noticed that the letterhead had Dr. Stoltz's name grouped together with other physicians under the office name WestPoint Neurological Clinic. The third sheet of paper in the stack was not a bill at all but a medical report. For a cranial MRI. For a Mr. Chase Thompson.

"What?" Alexa gasped in shock. Why would Chase have had brain imaging without letting her know? With an uneasy feeling in her stomach, Alexa read on in an effort to make sense of what she had discovered. The test results were from several weeks ago.

Phrases such as *abnormal brain tissue*, *dark holes*, and *juxtacortical brain lesions* jumped off the page and clutched Alexa's heart. The report ended with the following line:

IMPRESSION: The findings are highly suggestive of multiple sclerosis.

The paper in Alexa's hand dropped silently to the floor.

* * *

December 17
Challenge #3—Be humble: be easily entreated, be respectful, and refrain from judging

Well, gang, we have made it to day 3! It has been awesome so far to read about your experiences and how accepting Grandpa's challenge has brought the Christmas spirit more fully into our lives.

Today's challenge appears to be simple, but I think it will be harder to put into practice in everyday life. I've realized since reading this challenge that I probably judge others much more than I realize.

The importance of this idea comes up a lot in Grandpa's writing, so I thought that for today's post, I'd include one of his journal entries written several months before he died. Here it is:

"One of my favorite authors has suggested that we 'assume the good in others and doubt the bad.' Why is it in mankind's nature to automatically read bad intentions into the actions of those around them? What if we all just made an effort to remember that the loved ones around us are probably doing the very best they can? I know I hope for—am even desperate for—this kind of mercy from my friends and family. So why wouldn't I extend it to others in return?"

Good luck today, my friends. Looking forward to reading about your experiences tonight! Don't forget to come back and post!

~Jacob

As Jeremy finished reading Jacob's latest blog post, he transferred it into a Microsoft Word document, then pushed the Print button to make a copy of it for Mrs. White because she didn't have access to the Internet in her little apartment. Jeremy had enjoyed hand-delivering the challenges every morning, as well as reading her the different blogpost responses each night from his phone. And she didn't seem at all disappointed in the more frequent visits the challenges were causing.

As Jeremy rang Mrs. White's doorbell, the smell of warm baked goods wafted out from under her doorway.

"Hello there, dear," she greeted Jeremy as she swung open her door. "You arrived just in time for some homemade gingerbread. Can I get you a slice with some fresh whipped cream?"

"Well, I guess the polite thing to do *would* be to accept," Jeremy teased as he bent down to give the elderly woman a gentle hug. "And how are you this morning, Meemaw?" he asked, using an affectionate name he had adopted for her over the years. Mrs. White had definitely become much more of a mother or grandmother to Jeremy than an employer, and he felt her name should reflect her special place in his life.

"Well, I felt good enough to bake you something special bright and early, now didn't I?" she said with a twinkle in her eye. "So what have you got for me today? I've felt giddy as a school girl all morning, wondering what Mr. G had in mind for day three."

Jeremy eagerly accepted the plate of warm gingerbread Meemaw handed him, then made himself at home at her old Formica kitchen table. "Jacob's post today not only included his grandpa's third challenge but words from the man himself. Here, I'll read it to you now."

Meemaw leaned back in her chair with her eyes closed as Jeremy read to her, drinking in the latest post like she was listening to a symphonic melody. "Assume the good, and doubt the bad," she repeated after he had finished. "I like that. A lot. Definitely harder to do than it looks."

"For some maybe," Jeremy countered. "But for people like me who have been misjudged and marginalized by others for most of their life, it's not as hard to be nonjudgmental toward others. Life has taught me there is more to a person than meets the eye."

"That is true, my dear boy," Meemaw agreed soberly. "You know as well as any person that we never know what someone has gone through in their lives—or is going through in their heart." The frail, ethereal-looking woman gazed out the window for a moment, focusing intently, although whether it was upon an object outside or a ponderous thought within, Jeremy could not tell.

She then broke the silence with a question. "And how is Jeanie enjoying this challenge?"

Jeremy shifted uncomfortably in his chair, wolfing down his final bite of gingerbread. Jeanie was a sore subject for him these days. Ever since her mother died, Jeanie had seemed less and less like the vibrant woman he had married. It was as though everything she looked at was now tinged with gray. "Oh, I don't know," he replied, feigning a yawn. "I'm not sure how much she's tried to do it. I don't know if she is all that into it."

"Oh really? What makes you say that?"

"Just a feeling I got, is all. She knows how much Mr. G meant to me, so she hasn't said anything outright. But just the way she was talking about it, I could tell she thought his suggestions were too . . . I don't know . . . simple, I guess. She just seemed a little doubtful is all. But then that's kind of how she's been about a lot of things lately. She's just been really . . . different . . . since her mother died."

"Trials have the ability to change us, that's for sure," Meemaw said. "I've been there myself. When Mr. G moved into this complex, it was a very miserable time in my life—widowed, lonely, and no children or grandchildren to call my own. It seemed like God had kept every good thing from me and I could find nothing to hope for. But what I couldn't see was that my self-pity was destroying me." She shifted her gaze from outside to looking deep into Jeremy's eyes. "But Mr. G's friendship changed me. He brought the hope of the Savior back into my life. I started to understand that Jesus could help me carry my burdens. Soon I started thinking of others more and looking for the good. Negativism vanished, and hope grew in its place. It took time, my dear boy, but I made it through. And with lots of love and patience, your Jeanie will too."

Jeremy returned her gaze but kept silent for a moment, pondering her words as they hung in the air. Then he stood from the table and leaned over to give his friend a peck on the cheek. "Oh, Meemaw, if I only had half your wisdom. Thanks for a great start to my morning."

"No, thank *you* for coming by," she said, smiling up at him warmly, though Jeremy caught a touch of worry in her eyes. "I really appreciate you delivering these daily challenges from Mr. G. It's done my heart such good. How about me showing my gratitude by having you and your family come over for dinner tonight? How does homemade chicken pot pie sound?"

Jeremy pushed the door open with conflicting feelings in his heart. *Isn't it Jeanie who needs to change? She's the one carrying around all the negativity and anger, not me!* Then he remembered the day's challenge: *Be humble and refrain from judging.* "Well, today's challenge is taking an unexpected turn," he murmured under his breath.

"What was that, sweetie?" Meemaw called out from behind him. "Was that a yes on dinner?"

"Sure, Meemaw, we would love it. And Jeanie will be thrilled to have someone else cook tonight. Now there's some good news for her," he joked as he slipped out the door. Sure, it was just a dinner invitation, but he hoped that any positive news coming Jeanie's way might help.

* * *

Maggie logged on to her laptop, eager to read about everyone's experiences of the day. Because Jacob was still at a late-night basketball practice, Maggie was unable to check in on how his day had gone, but at least she could read what was going on with the others.

And maybe, if she felt brave enough, she would share a little of her own good news.

The blog was surprisingly quiet, even empty-feeling, tonight. The last post was Jacob's, announcing the challenge that morning. Maggie wondered if today's challenge was harder for the group to pull off than the first two. Maybe that was why they had so little to say.

For her, it had been quite a positive experience. And once again, this exercise had had its greatest effect on her relationship with her coworker Zach. Instead of ignoring him or, even worse, being suspicious of his efforts to lend her a hand, she realized he was in actuality just a very helpful person. She found herself softening toward his efforts to help around the office and felt her cheeks warm a bit as she remembered how he looked at her when she thanked him at the end of their workday.

Should she post tonight about her latest discoveries? As Maggie considered the new emotions stirring within her, she decided to keep silent for the time being. *What if I'm making a bigger deal out of this than it really is? It's hard to say, but I have to admit the mystery of it all adds to the excitement.* With a hot mug of cocoa in hand, she sat in front of the glow of their Christmas tree lights and felt the hope of the season fill her heart.

* * *

December 17

Challenge #3—Be humble: be easily entreated, be respectful, and refrain from judging

From Alexa: I don't know how all of you tackled this overwhelming virtue, but this has been an eye-opener for me. After a long (and difficult) day pondering this challenge, I've decided that humility is not only essential but the introductory virtue for all change—especially if you want to help other people change too. This isn't for a day. This virtue is a starting point for life and all of our relationships. If there is any pride or selfishness, we are doomed.

Sometimes we hold things in, and we are afraid to risk our innermost thoughts for fear we will make ourselves seem weak or unable to cope by ourselves. If we embrace everything with a humble heart, which is being easily entreated and teachable, we can grow together whether it is in a marriage relationship or with a coworker. We have to respect each other's needs, frailties, and trials. Withholding judgment is a must because everybody's hearts are different and all need nurturing and love! Thank you, Mr. G, for helping us along the way long after you departed.

Well, I just had to spill my heart out. I hope it made sense.

~Alexa

* * *

After finishing reading Alexa's post, Chase closed his laptop and stood to leave the office. He had put in a late night and felt weary in body and spirit. His heart was toggling between both hope and dread. Alexa's words were so heavy. Had she discovered his secret? But how? And yet her post was also so merciful. Could she possibly forgive him for hiding it in the first place?

Chapter Four
LET US REJOICE AND BE GLAD

Jacob awoke to the sound of his mom singing "Oh What a Beautiful Mornin'" from *Oklahoma!* downstairs. From the smoky, sweet aroma that filled his room, he guessed she was probably cooking an early-morning breakfast that involved bacon—Jacob's favorite. Clearly Grandpa's ten-day challenge was having an effect on his mother. She'd been positively glowing these past few days.

Remembering the blog, Jacob jumped up from bed, then winced in pain. His muscles cried out in rebellion against the intense basketball conditioning he'd undergone the night before. In fact, he was so exhausted by the time he'd returned home that he had fallen right into bed without checking the website.

Before posting the day's new challenge, Jacob took a minute to read through the responses from the night before. He was excited to see that the group was still motivated to meet each daily challenge. And yet he wondered at Alexa's response. It was thought-provoking, for sure, but also ponderous. The challenge for day four would lighten everyone's mood a bit. *Not that Mom needs any help in that area*, he joked to himself.

December 18

Challenge #4—Be happy: choose to be of good cheer, laugh a little, and share it with others

Every day gets better, doesn't it? A big thanks to Alexa for her thoughts on humility. I can just imagine my grandpa looking down with joy as he watches his experiment being fulfilled. He really wanted to help everyone around him be happy.

I found this scribbled in the margin of one of his journal pages, and it reminded me of day 2: "It is hard to find happiness until you have become acquainted with gratitude." I'm starting to realize that the two—gratitude and happiness—are inseparable.

That brings us to challenge #4: Choose to be happy. I can hardly wait for today's adventures! Matthew and I have the greatest idea we hope to pull off. Can't wait to report on it later!

The Christmas List 43

Nothing like Christmastime to get you in the spirit of bringing a little happiness into another person's life. That's what Grandpa tried to do with his coded cards.

Let's all get out there and sprinkle around a little Mr. G cheer!

Have a happy day!

~Jacob

Because their charter school served grades K–12, Jacob and Matthew were blessed to spend time together every day. In addition to occasionally seeing each other in the hallways or lunch room, they met every day after school in the library to pass the next hour and a half doing homework or reading before one of their parents picked them up to take them home.

Today's library experience was going to be a bit different. At least he hoped it would be. Much of it depended on the person at the library whom everyone feared the most—the head librarian, Ms. Johnson.

Old Ms. Johnson's presence loomed large in that little library. Ever present at her antique wooden desk central to the building's layout, Ms. Johnson always had her eye on *everybody* and a tight handle on *everything*. From the noise level to the books that were less than twenty-four hours overdue, Ms. Johnson controlled it all and everyone knew her as No-Mercy Johnson.

No-Mercy Johnson's appearance didn't help matters either. Her glossy skin seemed to stretch so tightly across her face that it looked ready to split if even slightly provoked. Jacob figured that must have been what prevented her from ever smiling, coupled with her obvious annoyance with students and, well, everyone. Her hair was perpetually styled in a dated, wash-and-set hairdo, the color of which could only be described as varmint brown-gray. To make matters worse, the clothing she wore was always dark and heavy, reminiscent of a cloak that could both conceal her form and darkly intimidate those around her.

But today Jacob and Matthew would not run *from* her but *to* her. Mr. G's challenge had invited them to spread some cheer, and they could think of no one else who seemed to need it more than Ms. Johnson. From the moment Jacob had discovered his grandpa's ten challenges, Ms. Johnson had entered his mind as someone he should focus on. And today's invitation to spread happiness seemed to beg for no needier recipient.

One of Jacob's merit-badge requirements was to help someone begin the process of researching their family history. In a flash of inspiration, Jacob had had the idea that he and Matthew could provide this little service for Ms. Johnson. That is, if she'd allow it. Jacob was banking on the fact that the older generation always seemed to love genealogy, and he hoped Ms. Johnson would be flattered by the attention.

Jacob walked through the library doors that afternoon mustering all the confidence and genuine cheer he possibly could and had a more-intimidated Matthew hiding in his shadow.

Unsurprisingly, Ms. Johnson's dark form was huddled over a book at her desk in the center of the room. Jacob quickened his pace to close the distance, silently reciting the lines he'd been practicing all day.

"Good afternoon, Ms. Johnson," he said brightly. "Do you have a few minutes today to help your local Scouting program? You see, I'm working toward earning my Eagle and—"

"Shhhhhhh!" she cut him off midsentence. "This is a library, young man. Would you please keep your voice down?" She stood, pushed up her glasses, and took a closer look at the boys. "Why, if it isn't Jacob Garcia. I seem to remember you have some grossly overdue books at the moment, do you not?"

Jacob flashed her a disarming smile, although the hint of fear in his eyes betrayed him. "I came prepared, Ms. Johnson," he said quickly, pulling out the worn copy of Dickens's *Christmas Carol* from his backpack. "It's actually not due until next week now—I renewed it online this morning—but I brought it back anyway. Better to be safe than sorry."

"I'll say," she snipped, whisking it from his hands and scanning the barcode to check it back in. "This book is in high demand right now."

Matthew coughed uncomfortably.

"Anyway," Jacob started up again, undeterred, although now speaking in a more careful whisper. "Like I was saying, in order to earn my genealogy merit badge, I need to help someone research the first few generations of their family line. Have you ever searched your family lines,

The Christmas List   47

Ms. Johnson?" he asked with a hopeful lilt. "It will only take a few minutes, and it can really be a lot of fun."

Ms. Johnson stood there silently, awkwardly for a moment, then finally stammered, "Y-you, you're talking about my family history, young man? You want to research *my family*? Well, I've never been asked such a question." Her expression seemed to soften a bit, and she looked at the two boys in front of her as if she was seeing them for the first time. And perhaps letting them see her for the first time too. "But I guess I don't see why not."

"That's great!" Jacob said as Matthew nodded beside him. "You'll be amazed at how simple it can be with the Internet. May we use your computer?"

Ms. Johnson looked around the empty library and seemed to conclude that now was as good a time as any. "Sure, boys, come on back here," she said, inviting them behind the desk.

Jacob and Matthew got to work, showing her how to use FamilySearch and several other helpful websites. To their surprise, quite a few of her generations had already been researched and completed. There was definitely a genealogy aficionado somewhere in her family.

"Why, I had no idea!" she exclaimed, then blushed, quickly lowering her voice to a barely audible whisper. "I can't believe all this information is just sitting here." Her eyes were glued to the computer monitor. "Look at all that family!"

"It's great, isn't it?" Matthew piped in, detecting the slightest smile on the librarian's face, which made him grin ear to ear.

Jacob couldn't help but notice Ms. Johnson's name alone on the screen. For some reason, her husband's and children's names had not been recorded next to hers. "Now, sometimes you'll find there can be missing information. But that's where you can fill it in yourself," he prompted her. "Does this look complete to you?"

She scrutinized her name, and all three of them seemed to hold their breath. "Yes, that about does it," she replied softly.

Jacob read her birth year and did the math. He was shocked to realize Ms. Johnson was only in her early forties. He'd assumed she was decades older than that, possibly even a grandmother already. Her gray-toned hair and old-fashioned clothing betrayed her; he couldn't believe she wasn't much older than his own mother.

Her gaze had moved from the computer screen to the window overlooking the grassy hills outside. "I was almost married . . . but I never did. My fiancé and I were in a terrible automobile accident the week before our wedding. We were hit head-on by a gasoline tanker, and . . ." With a pained look in her eyes, she trailed off. "Well, I came out of it badly burned but alive. But my Henry didn't make it." She glanced down at her hands uncomfortably and then said, "But all that was a long time ago, boys. And I best be getting back to work." She stood from the desk. "Still, thank you very much for taking a small interest in my life this afternoon and helping me take an interest in my family history again. Now run along. I'm sure you have plenty of homework to do."

Jacob wanted to run along—to get out of there fast and get back to his books and pretend nothing out of the ordinary had just happened. But he felt like he couldn't move. Suddenly it all made sense. Her tight, burn-scarred skin; her mousy-gray, unchanging hairstyle, which he now realized was a wig; and the heavy pain that seemed to color every interaction she had with those around her. Jacob swallowed hard at the lump in his throat and felt ashamed.

Though she was busy resuming her work, stacking books in her arms to reshelf in various areas, she paused and looked deeply into both boys' eyes. "You have blessed me with a wonderful afternoon, you two. It brought me great happiness to see all my family on that computer screen—to remember how much family I really do have. So thank you." She quickly turned away and walked toward the shelves across the room.

Matthew turned to Jacob excitedly. "She said the word, Jacob! She actually used the word *happiness*. It worked!"

"Yes, she did," Jacob replied soberly. "But saying the word *happiness* once is not enough. All I can think of now is how to bring her more of it."

* * *

The Christmas List 51

Challenge #4—Be happy: choose to be of good cheer, laugh a little, and share it with others

8:45 p.m.—Comment #1

From Maggie: What a day this turned out to be! What seemed to start out as a total failure to meet today's challenge ended very unexpectedly.

At lunchtime I left to pick up sandwiches for the office, only to find I couldn't because my car wouldn't start! Having just replaced the brakes last month, I don't think I need to go into how unhappy I was. After unsuccessfully trying to jumpstart my battery for the next 15 minutes, Zach kindly offered to run the errand himself. Still, that gesture didn't do much to dissipate the dark storm cloud that loomed over my head the rest of the afternoon. I felt terrible because I knew I was supposed to be spreading good cheer—but no matter how hard I tried, I could only exude a cumulonimbus countenance.

Zach offered to take me home after work, even though I warned him we'd first have to pick up Jacob and Matthew from the school library. He stayed in the running car while I hurried in to get the boys. I was distracted and annoyed by this unexpected repair I would now have to pay for during the most expensive month of the year.

Then I was met by something that completely shocked me—a smiling Ms. Johnson. Shocked, because, as most of you know, she is the perpetually unhappy school librarian. She went on to gush about our "incredibly kind and thoughtful boys" who had introduced her to her family history online that afternoon. We talked for a few minutes about her experience—long enough that the boys soon joined us, as well as Zach, who, because of the delay, had parked the car and come in to see if he could help.

Aware of today's challenge, Zach proposed that we continue our happy gathering over dinner at a family buffet down the street. What a fun and unexpected evening this turned out to be! After we'd eaten ourselves into happy comas, Zach pulled out his phone for more family history investigating on his FamilySearch app. A little further inquiry revealed that Ms. Johnson's family lines had been traced all the way back to Mary Queen of Scots! Ms. Johnson had us all in stitches as she uncharacteristically stood and began to bow and curtsy before us like true royalty! The best part of the night was just outside the restaurant as we hugged and said good-bye. I saw in Ms. Johnson's eyes what looked to be pure and genuine happiness. What a sight!

Lastly, I thought you'd all enjoy reading a couple things I've found in Dad's journal that he wrote regarding happiness:

"If you've never been acquainted with gratitude, you will never know happiness."

"I know there is no happiness except in righteousness. I have proven that through my sorrowful life—although it can be found again through forgiveness."

And finally one that seems especially poignant after tonight: "Good relationships are the seedbed for happiness. When I lost my relationship with my wife and daughter, I lost any hope for real happiness. But through the goodness of God, I eventually came to taste the joy that forgiveness can bring."

* * *

Forgiveness. Joy. Happiness. The words were so sweet Chase could almost taste them. Yet they seemed just beyond his reach.

He closed his laptop and looked over at Alexa, lying next to him. Today's challenge had been just that for him—a challenge. Since the moment he'd awoken, he'd struggled to feel any happiness himself, let alone share it with others. Reading Mr. G's words just now was the first glimmer of joy he'd felt all day.

If he was honest with Alexa and could obtain her forgiveness, then in spite of his failing body, could he feel happiness once again?

He lifted his hand to tap her shoulder but then paused. The thought of breaking her heart to salve his own didn't sit right with him—at least not at this hour of the night. He'd wait one more day. He prayed that tomorrow he'd find the courage.

Chapter Five
EASY AS PIE

December 19
Challenge #5—Be encouraging: share praise, inspiration and encouragement

Your posts have been awesome! After yesterday's experience, I've decided I want to try to bring someone a little happiness every day—10-day challenge or not. Grandpa was right! We can make a difference in people's lives.

Today's challenge comes with a cool acronym Grandpa created—PIE. Try to give everyone you meet a little . . .
P raise
I nspiration
E ncouragement

You will be amazed at the big things these three little words can do.

Thanks for being so good. (Grandpa would like that little play on words, don't you think?)

Your pal,

~Jacob

"You know, today's challenge has triggered a memory—something I haven't thought about for some time," Chase told his family as they gathered around the breakfast table. "Matthew, when I was a little boy, I wanted to play basketball more than anything else. I had big dreams of playing college basketball, but did you know I didn't even make the team my freshman year of high school? I was devastated. The following year, I made JV, but I was never a dominant player. During my junior year, I played varsity but sparingly. I kept working hard to improve, but somehow I couldn't make the leap to my full potential."

Chase had Matthew's rapt attention. He continued. "One day a new coach, Don Snow, called me into his office and said, 'Chase, I've been watching you, and you're going to be a great ballplayer. With a few small changes, you could be my starting center and captain of the team. You can do this!'

"Something immediately sparked in my heart, and my game quickly improved. That year we won the state championship, and I was voted all-state. And eventually I was offered a scholarship to NYU, where I had great success playing college basketball. To think it all started with, 'Chase, you are going to be a great ballplayer.' And after reading Mr. G's acronym this morning, I understand why. I was praised, inspired, and encouraged to be better—and that is exactly what I became."

Matthew was amazed. It was the first time he'd heard the full story of his dad's great days as a college athlete. He couldn't wait to tell Jacob after school. And Ms. Johnson too. He had a feeling yesterday had sparked an ongoing friendship among the three of them.

* * *

As Matthew ran out to catch the bus, Alexa remained in her kitchen chair, pushing her scrambled eggs around her plate, deep in thought. Chase's words had flipped a light on in her mind. She'd gone through a whole range of emotions since finding that manila envelope—anger, hurt, fear, despair, and more anger still. But unleashing all that on her husband would do neither one of them any good. What Chase *really* needed right now was clear—pie.

"Chase," she said softly, "thank you for sharing that story. It reminds me of what a hard worker—what an excellent person—you have always been. You are a fighter, honey! And there is no setback, no weakness, no *sickness* that can change that."

Chase's breath caught in his throat. He looked searchingly into Alexa's eyes for a confirmation of what he already knew. "Alexa, I'm so sorry I—"

"No sorrys," she cut him off firmly. "We will waste no time hurting or blaming or pulling apart. We can fight this, but, honey, we must fight it *together*. In the words of Coach Snow, 'You can do this!' *We* can do this!"

Chase pushed his chair back to rise and hug his wife, but his legs would not cooperate. Sensing his struggle, Alexa jumped up to hug him, nearly falling into his lap. "Let me help you, honey. You don't have to do this alone."

He wrapped his arms around her and buried his face in her fragrant hair. *How dare I hide this from her for so long. Even worse, how dare I try to do this alone.*

Allowing himself to push aside the searing guilt for just a moment, he held her tighter.

* * *

December 19

Challenge #5—Be encouraging: share praise, inspiration, and encouragement

9:32 a.m.—Comment #1

From Jeremy: I was down and out. There weren't any gigs scheduled for my little hip-hop group. No money. No parents. No help. It was just a few days before the rent was due. And there was no hope! My little brother and my cousin depended on me. As the oldest, I was the leader, the boss, and the provider.

One day someone gave me a chance. I felt like I was dreaming! Someone actually wanted to help, even hire, me? Maybe I was worth something after all. I could do things. And each time I did, I was met with gratitude, praise, and continual encouragement. Now there was a little money in my pocket and food in the cupboard. But it didn't stop there. With this angel's help, I went back to school, secured a future for myself, and met my sweetheart, Jeanie.

Yes, you know this lady. Mrs. White's praise, inspiration, and encouragement changed my life. So when today's challenge came, I had to get on here and acknowledge that because of my meemaw's delicious home-cooked PIE, I am the man I am today. I love her and thank Mr. G too because he was the one who lit that fire of hope within her. Bless his soul.

Well, I'm on my way over to Mrs. White's apartment now to catch her up on today's challenge. Thanks, Jacob. You're the man. And so was your grandpa.

In a way, he feels like my grandpa too.

Love to all,

Jeremy

* * *

"This is the second night in a row you've fed me dinner, Mr. Jones. I fear I'm getting spoiled," Maggie said playfully. Gazing up at the winter sky as Zach walked her back to her doorstep, she was filled with the joy and wonder of the season. In fact, this season had been more wonderful than any she'd remembered in a long time.

"Well, after you told me Jacob would be at practice again until late tonight, I saw no reason for you to have to cook for one. Plus, you can't exactly say a dinner of Subway sandwiches could qualify as spoiling you."

They stopped in front of her door, and a wave of shyness washed over her. *You're in your forties, not fourteen! Stop making such a big deal about a week-old friendship and a couple meals with a nice employee.* But the intent look on Zach's face as he stood there in the twinkling porch light caused her heart to race.

"Maggie, I . . ." Zach trailed off but held her gaze. Rather than finishing his sentence, he gently reached for her hand. The warmth and energy of his grasp took Maggie by surprise, like lightning through a conductor. "Maggie, I know this seems sudden, but from a distance, for me at least, this has gone on much longer." He hesitated, searching for the words. "You are the most . . . incredible—"

The sound of a car pulling up made them both turn and look toward the street. The SUV door swung open, and Jacob hopped out, backpack and basketball in tow. "Hey, Mom. Coach ended practice early tonight," he called out as he ran up the walkway. "Hey, Mr. Jones! What are you guys up to?"

Jacob stopped short after his eyes darted to his mom's hand in Zach's. He flushed deeply, but his embarrassment must have quickly given way to a protective anger. "Mom, it's freezing! What are you doing standing out here in the cold?"

The irritated flash in her son's eyes surprised Maggie, and she instinctively pulled her hand away. "You're right, Jacob. We . . . we should go in." She looked back at Zach, then said rather formally, "You've been kind, Mr. Jones. A very considerate coworker indeed." Then she added lamely, "Thanks for the ride, and . . . and the sandwich."

Wanting to escape Zach's hurt expression as quickly as possible, Maggie slipped through the door without another word.

Chapter Six
HOLD ON—PAIN ENDS

December 20

Challenge #6—Be full of hope: Seek understanding. Live with hope for yourself and others.

Hello, wonderful friends, Maggie here. Jacob had to leave early this morning for some reason and asked that I write today's post.

So my dad's journal mentions today's topic often. On his door hung a little yellow card with the numbers 16-3-5-10. And of course you recognize those numbers as "hope."

He wrote this in his journal, "Hope is the greatest and most empowering virtue to help us carry on against the adversities and trials of life. Where there is no hope, life is dismal at best. Hope gives you the fortitude, resilience, and strength to move forward in the difficult moments. It not only enlivens the soul but also empowers the mind and releases the energy of the heart with great enthusiastic expectations. It gives you the power to see beyond the moment of discouragement to a brighter day. It is the power and strength of resilience—to get up and try again."

Wow, I don't know about you, but I really needed to hear that today. Life can be so complicated—living with hope is no easy task.

Remember to post tonight. They are always terrific. I'd love to hear more about how these challenges are affecting your Christmas season.

Sincerely,
~Maggie

* * *

December 20
7:40 p.m.—Comment #1

From Jeanie: I have to be honest. This has been hard for me. I was the lone person in our group who never knew Mr. G. You all were so full of enthusiasm to try this ten-day stuff, but I felt spiritually skeptical, even angry about life itself. I had lost hope.

Most of you may not know that I buried my mother earlier this year. I had prayed for her healing, but to no avail. When her body was lowered into that dark, cold grave, it was as if I was descending with her. Part of me died that day because she was

The Christmas List

the only constant I'd had throughout my life. Pity consumed my daily thoughts. Where was God when I needed Him?

But when I read about hope from Mr. G's journal today, it was as if something started to melt in my heart. This flame seemed to warm and fill me all morning. When Jeremy came home for lunch, I asked him for more details about Mr. G's story. I was deeply moved by his ability to carry on through such sorrow and regret for so many years. Hope must have been his lifeline that enabled him to carry on.

And so I started to think more deeply about hope and the darkness I'd allowed to consume me. Everyone has to die. No one lives forever. But I have a husband and future family I need to keep living for. My heart and mind have been awakened today, and I've felt the light of hope returning. Below are some thoughts that have come to me throughout the day.

Hope is a power to look for the good.

Hope is not just an optimistic attitude but a virtue that empowers us to carry on.

When I count my blessings, my hope increases.

Hope is the light of my life. Through it, I can see my path more clearly.

Hope can conquer adversity.

Hope makes me a positive person.

Hope helps me look up because there is help from above.

I can help others live with hope.

And then it dawned on me—another acronym:

Hold
On—
Pain
Ends

I feel like I'm realizing for the first time that the Christmas spirit is all about hope. Hope in the Son of God and that through Him ALL pain will one day end! I want the Christmas spirit to live in my heart every day of my life. Blessed be the name of Mr. G. I am alive again.

All my love,
~Jeanie

* * *

Alexa was beaming. "Chase, that was a beautiful response from Jeanie tonight, wasn't it? This message of hope could not resonate any more with me than it does right now. I am so full of it—for you, for us. Do you know what I learned today?"

"What did you learn today?" he asked her, straining to match her energy and enthusiasm.

Chase was sitting on the bedroom floor across from Alexa, theoretically there to help her wrap Matthew's presents behind closed doors, although Alexa had been chattering away with such excitement that she'd not even stopped to hand him anything to wrap. And it was just as well. It seemed as though every movement he tried to make today was mired in molasses.

"That diet and nutrition are huge factors when it comes to managing the symptoms and progression of MS. So eating raw and organic, a plant-based diet, fewer processed foods . . . I mean, these are all things we can easily do. I can help you with that, Chase. And more importantly, the Lord can help us with that—as long as we don't shut Him out."

Those last words stung. Shutting them out was exactly what he had done to both his sweet wife and the Lord. *How could I have turned away from the best friends I have? What kind of husband and disciple am I? Even though I'm no longer hiding the truth, why can't I feel any relief?*

The hope that the day's challenge invited seemed to elude him. He nodded in agreement with Alexa's words, but his heart didn't feel them. Perhaps for others, the pain could end, but his apparently would not.

Chapter Seven
A LANGUAGE THE DEAF HEAR, THE BLIND SEE

December 21

Challenge #7—Be kind and gentle: treat everyone with gentle kindness, especially the downtrodden

Christmas is almost here—and it's the most exciting one I can remember since I was a little boy. Somehow these daily challenges are bringing that magical feeling back into my heart. How could Grandpa know?

Perhaps you've noticed the little journal entries I've been trying to include from Grandpa to go along with each day's challenge. Again, with this next challenge, Grandpa has come through. I'll let him introduce challenge #7:

"Kindness is the true expression of love. Random acts of kindness are contagious, and through them there will be few you cannot reach. I love these words from Mark Twain: 'Kindness is the language which the deaf can hear and the blind can see.'"

Today my grandpa and your Mr. G has invited us to "be kind and gentle to those around us, especially the downtrodden." I can hardly wait to hear about your day.

Your friend,

~Jacob

After hitting Publish, Jacob closed his laptop and tucked it into his school bag. He would be late for school if he didn't hurry. Guilt tugged at his heart as he pecked his mom on the cheek and said good-bye. He didn't know why he'd reacted the way he did last night. It was just . . . his mom had never shown any interest in another man. And for some reason, Jacob had never even considered that a possibility and had never considered what it would mean for their little family.

But Grandpa's challenge made him want to smooth things over with her, even if nothing came of her friendship with Mr. Jones. He had to admit his mom had been much happier lately. Change was hard, but didn't she deserve it? He wracked his brain for what he could say to make things right. "Mom, I just want to say thanks for all that you've done for me. I could not have been raised in a better family. I love you."

* * *

Maggie sat in their now-silent kitchen, pondering what she'd just heard. Jacob's message had been loud and clear. He wanted to keep their little family of two exactly the way it had always been.

Although it seemed counterintuitive, her challenge to be kind today would require her to possibly hurt another person's heart. She could not deny what she had seen in Zach's eyes. And for the sake of her son, she had to let Zach know they could never be more than friends.

* * *

Jeremy and Jeanie had spent a delicious morning together. Jeanie felt as though the ice melting in her heart was making more room for her husband. She was saddened to realize how her pain had been shutting him out. It was humbling to realize how much they now owed to Mr. G. He had saved *both* of them.

Jeanie had been thinking of the movie *Pay It Forward* all morning and had some exciting thoughts to share with Jeremy. "Honey, let's find someone who is in a similar situation to what happened in the movie and be a secret benefactor. Someone who is downtrodden and without hope, like Mr. G has challenged."

Jeremy squeezed her. "That's it, Jeanie! What an amazing idea. I'll find a way to make it happen."

"Why don't you look for someone near your worksite—or even on it?" she suggested.

Jeremy agreed and decided to walk to work that morning. He prayed that his eyes would be opened so he could find someone along the way. He turned down a street he had never taken but realized quickly there was a reason for that. This was not a good part of town. Trash littered the streets and the smell of rotten garbage and destitute living filled the air.

Hearing a sudden scuffle behind him, Jeremy turned to see two young men in masks right behind him. The largest one held a metal pipe at the ready and whispered menacingly through clenched teeth, "Hand over your wallet *now* if you know what's good for you."

Before Jeremy could consider the consequences, he lunged at the thief and tackled him to the ground. The thief's metal pipe fell from his hand and rolled into the gutter. With a surge of adrenaline, Jeremy wrestled his arm around the man's neck and tried to pin him to the ground. The struggle had caused his attacker's mask to come off, and for one frightening moment, Jeremy stared into the man's dark and desperate face.

Suddenly Jeremy heard the sound of echoing metal as a searing pain shot through his brain. And then everything went black.

* * *

Jeanie choked back a wave of fear as she watched her husband lying there motionless on their couch. She knew he was in a pain-induced sleep and that, at the moment, that was the best thing for him. But seeing him this way suggested terrible scenarios of what could have been.

When Jeanie had received the phone call earlier that day from a local police officer, letting her know her husband had been found unconscious and was being transported to the nearest hospital, she'd felt as though time was standing still. Would there be yet another burial in her future? She was not sure she could bear it.

Much to her relief, once she arrived, the ER doctor explained that although Jeremy had suffered a slight concussion from the blow, he had no other injuries and, after a few hours of observation, could be released to go home.

A knock at the door startled Jeanie, pulling her from her thoughts. She opened the door to find a few friends from the Mr. G gang, love and concern radiating from them, bearing food and flowers and what looked to be a few packages.

"Oh, Jeanie," Mrs. White exclaimed, immediately encircling Jeanie in a comforting hug. "I hope you don't mind all of us barging in here. But as soon as Jeremy didn't show up today, I knew something was wrong. Once you told me what happened, I immediately called Maggie to see if she might accompany me here to check on you. And, of course, Jacob just had to come along too."

Maggie stepped inside and hugged Jeanie too, as best she could with the large bouquet and packages in hand. Then Jacob came up

The Christmas List 75

from behind with tasty-smelling bags hanging off his arms. "We are so relieved he's going to be okay," he said as he walked past the group to set his load in the kitchen.

Mrs. White's eyes welled up with tears at the sight of her boy, her Jeremy, there on the couch. "So they never found who did it?" she asked, her voice quivering with emotion.

"No, but thankfully they only made off with his cash. The police dogs found his wallet in a dumpster one street over with all his credit cards and other ID in place. Amazing!" Jeanie breathed, shaking her head. Then she continued. "Later on in the hospital, Jeremy was able to give a hazy description of one of the perpetrator's faces, which should help the police in the investigation. But they warned us that crimes like this are all too common in the neighborhood he was in and they may never find who did it."

"My word!" Mrs. White exclaimed. "Whatever was he doing in such a dangerous neighborhood?"

"Well, that's the irony," Jeanie said without bitterness but with rather deep admiration shining from her eyes. "He told me at the hospital he had chosen to go that route in hopes of the Lord guiding him to someone who needed his help . . . to the downtrodden, I guess you could say."

Maggie let out a little gasp. "How terrible, Jeanie! Does no good deed go unpunished?" she asked gently. "I'm just amazed this would happen with such a pure intent in mind."

"The Lord causes the rain to fall on the evil and the just, does He not?" Jeanie whispered with great faith. "I just thank Him with all my heart that my Jeremy is okay. But yes, the timing of this does emphasize how ironic life's challenges can be."

"That's not the only irony," Jacob said gravely, walking slowly into the room. "I don't know how to say this . . . but tomorrow's challenge may be our toughest one of all. Challenge 8 is going to ask us to forgive."

Chapter Eight
FORGIVENESS IS DIVINE

Saturday morning dawned, and Maggie arose early with the muted winter sun, hoping a walk around the neighborhood might help clear her thoughts. So much had happened yesterday; she wanted time to process it all before she dove into today's new challenge.

The look on Zach's face yesterday had proven impossible to erase from her mind. She accepted his invitation to go out to lunch with him only because of the window it would open for them to have an honest conversation about their relationship. She had tried to put it gently, but she'd let him know in no uncertain terms which relationship would come first in her life.

"I've enjoyed getting to know you better, Zach. Very much. But Jacob means the world to me. I have given him my life. And I just can't let anything—or anyone—come between us."

With both surprise and pain etched on his face, Zach's gentle response had shocked her.

"I know you've given him your life, Maggie, and in many ways, that's beautiful. But is that what he needs? For you to *not* have your own? No one will ever take that sacred place Jacob has in your life, but perhaps God has even more happiness in store for you."

Maggie was stunned by his choice of words—*more happiness in store*. She remembered recently wondering that very same thing. She had no answer for Zach and instead looked at her watch and said they needed to hurry back.

The drive back to the office was awkward and quiet. Maggie had almost spoken up several times but wasn't sure which would come out— an apology for her mistake or an angry epithet regarding his presumptuous observations about her life. Not wanting to risk either outcome, she kept silent.

Once they returned to the office, they were met immediately with the terrible news about Jeremy's incident, allowing Maggie's thoughts to focus on something completely different. She'd spent the rest of the afternoon getting updates from Jeanie and had left work early to prepare a few Christmas gifts and dinner for Jeremy and Jeanie.

Remembering Jeremy again this morning caused Maggie to step away from thoughts of Zach once again. Last night at Jeremy's apartment, she'd been so relieved to find he was not seriously injured and even more amazed to learn about his reaction to it all. Before she and the others had left their house that night, Jeremy had awoken for a few minutes and spoken with the group.

Even before hearing what the next day's challenge would be, Jeremy needed no prompting. Forgiveness was the first thing on his lips. "How can I hold a grudge against someone for doing something I might have done in the past myself? I have been that desperate, I'm afraid. And you know, I saw the look in my attacker's eyes, and as strange as it might sound, I feel sorry for him."

Maggie remembered the hurt look in Zach's eyes as she'd told him good-bye. She bit her lip now and felt tears well up in her eyes, hoping Zach could be just as forgiving.

* * *

December 22

Challenge #8—Be forgiving: mend a relationship and forgo a grudge

Jeremy's words and example last night make introducing the importance of today's challenge almost unnecessary. There are no words, Jeremy, except thank you! We hope you are feeling much better.

Grandpa too felt strongly about being forgiven and being forgiving. Having read and reread his journal, I know he yearned for forgiveness. My grandpa speaks reverently about the day when he knew he had been forgiven. No one could stop the tears from flowing. Grandpa recorded the following: "The capacity to forgive is one of the most divine attributes we can possess. I have heard it said that to be hurt is understandably human, but to forgive is divine.

"Forgiveness brings peace to the forgiver as well as to those forgiven. It is a sign of true strength, based on empathy and understanding.

"Forgiveness frees us from hurt, anger, and the desire for vengeance and retaliation. We are free of the burden of someone else's sin.

"As we consider the act of forgiveness, let us remember that mercy begets mercy. The Lord requires all of us to forgive. We can attain a remarkable degree of freedom and peace as we forgive others."

With the memory of Jeremy's example still fresh in our minds, let's prayerfully consider today who may be in need of our mercy.

Love to all,
~Jacob

* * *

Although there were only three days remaining until Christmas, Chase was determined to get at least one strand of Christmas lights hung. He'd been up early that morning to read the day's challenge, hopeful for more news on Jeremy's condition. The post had truly been inspiring, especially Jeanie's follow-up comments, which she'd posted immediately.

8:35 a.m.—Comment #1

From Jeanie: I echo your thoughts, Jacob. Jeremy has been an example to us all. For those of you who weren't there last night, he said of his attacker: "How can I hold a grudge against someone for doing something I might have done in the past myself? As strange as it might sound, I feel sorry for him."

Chase let those words roll around in his mind as he fought to hang the lights along the front porch, trying to get his arms to cooperate with the task at hand. He understood Jeremy's point; he really did. But what if the guilty person didn't deserve to feel that relief? What if what they did was so wrong they deserved to suffer and thereby realize what they had done?

He let out a frustrated yell as he struggled to undo a knot at the end of the strand. "C'mon! How has no one discovered a better way to make these things?"

"Daddy?" Matthew said, opening the door slowly. "Is everything okay?" He stood there, pajama clad and bleary eyed, with a worried but caring look in his eyes.

"Yes, son, I'm fine. Just trying to put these lights up is all." He forced a smile. "I'll survive, kiddo. Go on in and get some breakfast. I'll be done soon."

As Matthew shut the door, Chase silently berated himself for losing his temper. What was wrong with him these days? Participating in Mr. G's challenges had started out the season so well, but he couldn't help but notice that with each passing day, the Christmas spirit within him was diminishing.

Well, you did lie to your wife . . . and conceal some of the most life-altering news she could ever receive, he thought sarcastically. *Why should you be feeling the Christmas spirit? You don't deserve to feel that kind of joy.*

His mind returned to the thought that Jeremy's experience had triggered. *What if what the person did was so bad they deserved to suffer?*

Like waters clearing after the snow settles at the bottom of a Christmas globe, it suddenly became clear to Chase what his challenge for the day would be.

* * *

6:00 p.m.—Comment #2

From Chase: Yet again Mr. G's words have changed the course of my life.

I have to admit I have been struggling lately to feel the Christmas spirit. Instead of these challenges increasing that spirit in my life, it seems as though the reverse has been happening. And this has been very perplexing to me.

As I've pondered today's invitation to forgive, a person came to mind who has hurt me deeply. I hadn't realized how heavy the grudge was that I'd been carrying. But he had let me down so completely that it was hard not to hate him.

That person was me.

Several months ago, I was diagnosed with multiple sclerosis. Instead of turning to those who love me the most—my Heavenly Father and my sweet wife—I decided to hide it and hold the pain in. I told myself I'd eventually let Alexa know, but each day, as I felt my body deteriorate, I kept the devastating diagnosis to myself and tried to be strong.

Alexa was forced to find out the news on her own—and that I had hid it from her. And since our conversation last week when I finally had to face her (as well as the man in the mirror), I have not been able to forgive myself.

But why should I? I've argued in my mind. Shouldn't I hold on to this self-loathing longer in order

The Christmas List

to truly pay for what I have done? And yet in so doing, I've only forced those around me to continue to suffer just as much.

Reading Mr. G's words this morning—Forgiveness brings peace to both the forgiver and the forgiven—made me realize something ironic. I was both people! And also guilty of withholding peace from both.

And so I say to you all, my family, and my Father in Heaven that I am truly sorry. And not only am I sorry, but I am also ready to receive the Lord's forgiveness. I know this is what He wants for all of us. And I can truly say for the first time in a while that I feel His peace.

Merry Christmas,

~Chase

Chapter Nine
HELPING THE POOR AND NEEDY

December 23

Challenge #9—Be helpful to the poor and needy: seek to bless their lives

Well, we are coming to the end of this experience. And I know I'm not the only one who has been affected by it. Tomorrow is Christmas Eve, and, wow, does it feel like it! I can't remember the last time I felt this excited about the holiday season.

Today's challenge invites us to seek out specifically the poor and the needy. I don't know about you, but this seems like the very heart of the Christmas spirit. Maybe it's because I've basically grown up on the retelling of Dickens's *Christmas Carol* each year, but no Christmas season feels complete without reaching out to the less fortunate in some way or another.

Grandpa shared such a cool thought from his journal about this: "What is it about the Christmas season that makes us want to ensure the well-being of others? We could just be content to enjoy it by ourselves and with loved ones around us. What then makes us also turn to the stranger, the needy, and the less fortunate? Could that be what the angels foretold—that the Savior's birth would bring 'peace on earth and good will toward men'? I have found that the pure love Jesus puts in our hearts inevitably leads us to love and help others. Maybe good will means we are suddenly and miraculously now willing to do good."

Great food for thought, Grandpa. And thanks to all of you for being so willing.

Good luck out there today.

~Jacob

* * *

After he finished reading the post out loud, Jeremy looked up and smiled at Meemaw. "*Willing* to do good, huh . . . I like that."

"Oh my, I'll say," she agreed. "And I know just the family I want to help. They've recently moved in two doors down. I'm so thankful to you for coming over here each day to read these daily challenges to me. Especially today, so soon after your injury. Are you sure you're feeling well enough to be out and about?"

The Christmas List

"Now, Meemaw. A knock on the head was all it was. And besides, I was going out anyway for church, so it was just as easy to stop by here before the service. Don't you worry about me. I'm feeling much better already."

Jeremy rose from his chair to kiss her head of snowy white hair. "Well, I should be off if I'm going to make it on time."

Meemaw reached up and squeezed Jeremy's hand. "Thanks again, my sweet boy. So I'll see you tomorrow afternoon?"

"Yep, for our traditional Christmas Eve dinner. Wouldn't miss it for the world! That or your famous pumpkin pie."

Moments later, as Jeremy pushed open the apartment building's heavy glass doors, he stepped outside and inhaled deeply. The smell of wet pine and holiday baking filled the air. The world seemed to be at peace yet on the verge of a great celebration all at the same time.

* * *

"Do you recognize that woman over there?" Jeanie whispered to her husband as she nodded her head toward the end of their pew and flipped the hymnal to the final congregational carol.

There sat an older woman, her head bowed, quietly wiping her face with a handkerchief. Her wool overcoat appeared dingy and threadbare, and her salt-and-pepper hair was pulled back into a loose bun that looked slept in and in need of a washing.

Jeremy shook his head no as they began the hymn. The second verse touched him in a way it never had before.

> *He came down to earth from heaven,*
> *Who is God and Lord of all,*
> *And His shelter was a stable,*
> *And his cradle was a stall;*
> *With the poor, and mean, and lowly,*
> *Lived on earth our Savior holy.*

Jeremy could hardly wait for the hymn to end and was up out of his pew as soon as the amens were said. Mr. G had challenged them to seek out the needy—the very ones the Savior had chosen to live among—and Jeremy could not deny the compelling urgency he felt to meet this woman.

Once he approached her, he stood awkwardly for a moment, realizing he hadn't a clue what to say. "Merry Christmas, ma'am," he finally managed to get out. "Wonderful service, wasn't it?"

She looked up in surprise, her eyes moist with emotion. She held his gaze but said nothing.

Jeanie came up behind him and smoothed over the exchange. "Let us introduce ourselves. My name is Jeanie, and this is my husband, Jeremy. We have not yet had the chance to make your acquaintance," she said easily with a warm smile.

The woman seemed to relax a bit and then spoke quietly. "Yes, well, this is my first time here. Can't say I'm much of a churchgoer, except for around this time of year. But I was raised to do as much, and it doesn't seem right to stay home on the Sunday before Christmas, now does it?" Her cheeks flushed a deep red, and she looked away uncomfortably. "My name is Peggy Hart, by the way. Pleased to meet you."

She stood and maneuvered into the aisle. "Well, I better hurry home before that storm hits that they've predicted. Wouldn't want to be caught on foot in that mess." She politely nodded her head to them, and then, with an expression that seemed filled with appreciation, she said, "Thank you for introducing yourselves. Have a Merry Christmas."

"Wait, Ms. Hart," Jeremy said. "Please . . . allow us to drive you home. It would be no trouble for us at all."

Peggy again appeared uneasy. "No, no, I couldn't put you out. It's not far, and I really don't mind walking."

The three of them watched as fellow churchgoers dashed out of the building and into the pouring rain, racing to their cars. Peggy let out a little gasp and then an embarrassed giggle. "On second thought . . ."

Jeremy and Jeanie laughed along with her. "I sure hope you'll reconsider now," Jeremy said. "Here, let me run out and pull the car up for both of you. No drenched ladies on my watch!"

Moments later, Jeremy pulled up in their sedan, holiday carols playing and the heater blowing nice and warm. "My, my, the royal treatment," Jeanie teased. "Our carriage awaits."

Peggy entered the backseat hesitantly and thanked them again. "This is very kind of you. And I won't make you drive me all the way back home. To my side of town would be fine. Believe me, I'm used to walking. And a little rain don't hurt nothin'. I live over by the old saw mill, if you know where that is."

"Sure do," Jeremy answered. "I'm working on a jobsite in that area."

"Well, then, you are blessed, sir," Peggy replied quietly. "Not everyone is as fortunate. To have work, that is."

After a somber moment of awkward silence, Jeanie chimed in again. "Do you live alone, Peggy? Do you have any children?"

Jeremy wondered if those questions might be too personal.

"Yes, I live with my two sons, who are older now. Thank goodness, I have them around to support me. Well, you know . . . at least . . . at least they try," she stammered. "Work has been hard for them to come by lately."

As they drove along, Jeremy couldn't help but notice that the houses started to look a lot older and the neighborhoods more dilapidated.

"You can just drop me off here at the corner market," Peggy said. "It's not far from here, and I need to pick up a few things before I get home."

"Oh, we don't mind waiting at all, Ms. Hart. This is not a light rainfall, you know. You'll get drenched!" Jeanie insisted. "Don't worry, we're not in any hurry. Pick up what you need, and then we'll just take you the rest of the way."

Peggy chose not to argue the point. "You're too kind. Let's just skip the store, then. Maybe I'll venture out later if this rain ever stops. You can turn right here on this street. I'm at the end of it on the left."

As they pulled in front of her house, it became clear to Jeremy why their new friend had tried so hard to avoid this moment. The worn fence around her yard had completely fallen over, the front steps were missing most of their slats, it seemed, and the tiny house itself seemed to slump to one side as if the roof was caving in. It looked nearly inhabitable or, at the very least, abandoned.

Peggy quickly filled the silence. "The old place needs a bit of work, but it's still home. The funny thing is that my sons have the know-how to repair it. Construction's what they do for a living. But materials take funds, and when it comes to that or food on the table . . ." She trailed off and opened her door. "Well, thanks again to the both of you. You've been very kind."

Jeremy hopped out and ran around to her side before she could decline. "Here, hook your arm in mine and let me walk you to the door. I'd never forgive myself if you slipped in all this rain."

"Merry Christmas, Ms. Hart," Jeanie called out to her as she watched the two of them navigate the badly cracked walkway.

Before they'd even reached the front door, Jeremy's thoughts were racing with ideas about how he might help this family in need. He had been so moved during the hymn by the thought of the "poor, and mean, and lowly" that it was as if the Lord had led him right to this family.

He reached for the handle, but the door was already beginning to swing open. Someone must have seen them coming. Her son's tall frame suddenly filled the doorway.

Jeremy looked him in the eyes and began to introduce himself when he suddenly stopped dead in his tracks. Nothing could have prepared him for what he saw—he was looking once again into the eyes of his attacker.

Chapter Ten
GO ABOUT DOING GOOD

Chase pulled on his old work boots he'd retrieved from the garage, but he was lost in thought about Jeremy's post from the night before.

It was unbelievable, nearly impossible.

Not just the part about Jeremy being led *physically* but also the part about his being led *spiritually*.

Chase looked out his bedroom window and watched lavender dawn break on the valley below. *Christmas Eve.* And an unforgettable one it would be, at that, he was sure.

He crossed the room and grabbed his laptop off the nightstand, getting back online to reread Jeremy's response to challenge #9.

9:25 p.m.—Comment #3

From Jeremy: Interesting how we can pray and ask God to lead us but we are not always prepared to follow through with where that path might go. How I hope I will always be ready!

Today at church, after the service, with challenge #9 in mind to care for the poor, I felt strongly that I should approach a woman I'd never before met. Jeanie and I drove the woman home and found her living in quite desperate conditions.

I walked her to the door, and her son answered it. You can imagine my shock when I found myself looking at the very person who had mugged me the other day.

He excused himself immediately and bolted out of the room, and I stood there in shock as his mother apologized for his abrupt behavior.

I surprised myself even more as I spoke the words God put into my mouth: "Ms. Hart, I know we just met, but for more reasons than one, I feel that God has led me to your family. It is because of this that I ask you to not turn down what I'm about to propose."

I then told her about you all—my amazing friends who were looking for ways to serve this Christmas. And how, thanks to my work, I have building supplies readily available.

"How about we come by tomorrow to fix a few things around your house? This will mean more to us—to me—than you know," I heard myself saying to her. And I meant it.

She didn't quite know how to respond, but, then, I didn't give her the chance either. I told her we'd be back in the morning and left without waiting for her reply.

So, friends, if any of you are willing and able to continue our goal to help the needy, please join me tomorrow at the address below. I plan on being there from about eight to noon.

And as for any further plans I might have for this family God has led me to, I'm just praying He'll continue to show me the way.

Your brother in love,

~Jeremy

* * *

Jacob and Maggie were up early that Christmas Eve morning. Maggie needed to start some of the baking for their holiday dinner before they went to Jeremy's service project, and Jacob wanted to make his final post on the blog.

As Maggie began mixing the dough for the homemade rolls, Jacob joined her in the kitchen for a quick bowl of cereal.

"What a wonderful Christmas Eve we have in front of us," Maggie beamed as she wiped flour on her patchwork apron. *There's only one thing missing*, she thought wistfully to herself, then quickly pushed those thoughts out of her mind. *No, I will not spoil this holiday feeling sorry for myself*, she resolved.

"So true, Mom. Isn't it amazing what Jeremy has put together?" Then, as if reading her mind, Jacob added, "Although it'd be even better if we got more people in on the joy. Hey, we should call Zach to see if he could help us out this morning."

It was the first time Jacob had mentioned him since their strained exchange the other night. Maggie was shocked to hear her son bring his name up and wondered if he was testing her. "Oh, I'm not sure Zach would be able to join us on such short notice. Besides, I don't think he and I will do a lot together from now on."

"Really?" Jacob looked genuinely surprised. "Why, Mom? You guys seemed to really enjoy each other's company. Look, Mom, if this is because of the other night, well . . . I was just a little surprised, that's all. But I never intended for you to stop your life for me. To tell you the truth, I've become much more used to the idea of you dating. It actually makes me happy to think of you not having to be alone. You deserve that."

Maggie didn't know what to say. The thought of seeing Zach again, of giving it another go, made her heart skip a beat. "I don't know," she suggested through a shy smile. "Maybe I could just call him to see what he's up to today. Couldn't hurt, I guess."

"Nope, couldn't hurt at all," Jacob agreed with a wide smile. "Could not agree more."

* * *

December 24
Challenge #10—Be like our Savior Jesus Christ, and go about doing good.

Grandpa wrote, "The key to having the Christmas spirit—and, more importantly, a good life—is charity. For it never fails.

"'Charity suffereth long, and is kind; charity envieth not; charity vaunteth not itself, is not puffed up, Doth not behave itself unseemly, seeketh not her own, is not easily provoked, thinketh no evil; Rejoiceth not in iniquity, but rejoiceth in the truth; Beareth all things, believeth all things, hopeth all things, endureth all things. Charity never faileth: but whether there be prophecies, they shall fail; whether there be tongues, they shall cease; whether there be knowledge, it shall vanish away…And now abideth faith, hope, charity, these three; but the greatest of these is charity'" (1 Corinthians 13:4–8, 13).

After this scripture, Grandpa wrote, "The Good Book has the answers to a good life."

He then ended with this poem, which really sums up all ten of his challenges.

I am the Christmas Spirit—

I enter the home of poverty, causing palefaced children to open their eyes wide, in pleased wonder.

I cause the miser's clutched hand to relax and thus paint a bright spot on his soul.

I cause the aged to renew their youth and to laugh in the old glad way.

I keep romance alive in the heart of childhood, and brighten sleep with dreams woven of magic.

I cause eager feet to climb dark stairways with filled baskets, leaving behind hearts amazed at the goodness of the world.

I cause the prodigal to pause a moment on his wild, wasteful way and send to anxious love some little token that releases glad tears—tears which wash away the hard lines of sorrow.

I enter dark prison cells, reminding scarred manhood of what might have been and pointing forward to good days yet to be.

I come softly into the still, white home of pain, and lips that are too weak to speak just tremble in silent, eloquent gratitude.

In a thousand ways, I cause the weary world to look up into the face of God, and for a little moment forget the things that are small and wretched.

I am the Christmas Spirit

(E. C. Baird)

I have no doubt that every one of us has been changed by the experience of implementing these ten challenges. I would even go as far as to say that the course of our lives has been affected.

Grandpa was right about the heart of the Christmas spirit and also about the heart of life itself.

Let's make sure his legacy lives on by keeping these ten invitations at the heart of our lives the entire year long!

Your friend,

~Jacob

***

Chase and Alexa pulled up to the Hart property at the same time as Jeremy and Jeanie. "Couldn't have asked for a prettier morning," Chase commented cheerfully as he hopped out of his sedan and started pulling out two-by-fours from the back of Jeremy's truck.

"Low forties and sunny skies—I'll say!" Jeremy returned, stepping out of his pickup. "I'm thinking Mr. G had something to do with that."

"I wouldn't doubt it," Alexa said, closing her car door and hurrying around to the other side to grab the wood from Chase. She winked. "I'll take those, thank you very much." She started in the direction of the front yard, then called behind her, "Jeremy, this wood is for the fence, I'm assuming. Should I bring it over there?"

"Yes, ma'am," Jeremy confirmed, then looked at Chase with a more sober expression. "It looks like she's got your back, my friend."

"Yes, let's just say I'm realizing the power of teamwork. I'm sure there's nothing we can't do together." Chase let his gaze rest on his wife for a moment, then turned back to Jeremy and said, "I really respect what you're doing for this family, Jeremy. Have you confronted Ms. Hart's sons yet?"

"No," Jeremy shook his head. "In fact, she has no idea. I just had that one glimpse of her son before he left. They might not even be here today. Who knows? But either way, I've made peace with it. I won't say anything about it to them or their mother. The past is in the past. They are in obvious need, and I just want to help them in whatever way I can."

The Hart's front door swung open, and Ms. Hart's sons made their way down the dilapidated front-porch steps. The taller one strode across the lawn to close the distance between them, his expression full of pain and penitence. "Mister, please, you don't have to do this. It was awfully kind of you to offer, but we don't deserve this. My mom doesn't realize the things we've had to do to make ends—"

Jeremy held up his hand to cut him off. "There's no need to explain. I've been there myself. And that's why I want to help. Just pitch in today with what we do—that's all I ask."

The rough-looking young man stood there, speechless. "The money . . . I . . . well, I don't have it anymore. But I can—"

Jeremy cut him off again, extending his hand to shake his attacker's. "Let's make a deal. You and your brother are in construction, right? How about you pay it off by working on my jobsite for a while? And who knows? If I like what I see, I might just keep you around."

Now the young man was really dumbfounded, as was his younger brother, who was standing behind him listening to the exchange. No one could deny the pure Christlike love that permeated their entire group.

"But for now, we got work to do, boys," Jeremy boomed with a smile. "No more standing around, and that goes for all of you," he teased, looking around at his beloved friends.

Ms. Hart, wrapped in a tattered coat and an ear-to-ear smile, walked out onto the porch . "You heard him, boys. It's Christmas Eve! We've got celebrating to do and no time to waste." After she set down some mugs and a thermos of cocoa on the porch for everyone to enjoy, she wiped at her eyes.

Everyone turned as Maggie pulled up.

"Zach, nice to see you!" Chase called out as he saw his colleague exit the car with Maggie and Jacob.

Zach smiled and grabbed Maggie's hand, helping her over the muddy ditch to the front walkway. "Yeah, well, it's nice to be seen," he returned, joy shining in his eyes. "You don't think I'd miss the party, do you?"

"Not when you consider the guest list," Jacob quipped, winking at the two of them. He joined the group that had congregated on the lawn and said, "Well, Jeremy, everyone, this is amazing! I can't think of a better way to spend day ten, not to mention Christmas Eve, than with all of you, doing good. Thanks so much for putting this together."

Jeanie beamed at her husband and said, "Remember, Jacob, you're the one who gathered us to accomplish challenge #1 without any of us even realizing it. I think it's only right that my husband return the favor by helping us reunite here today."

Maggie beamed and looked upward for a moment, then whispered, "And I have a feeling we are not the only ones here today, my friends."

The heavens smiled down, and the Christmas spirit flooded the yard as the group got to work "doing good."

Author's Note

The ten ways to recapture the Christmas Spirit isn't something to do just for Christmas—it is something to do for the rest of our lives. This is the way the Savior taught us to live. And in that way, we will live after the manner of happiness.

The ten things Mr. G listed were teachings of Christ.

—A friend loves and cares for another even as Christ cared for us, for we are His friends (see John 15:15).

—Have a grateful heart. Express gratitude and thanksgiving in all things, and express it again and again (1 Thessalonians 5:18). Give thanks unto God (see Psalm 106:1).

—Be humble and easily entreated so change can occur (see Matthew 23:12; James 4:10), remembering always to never judge another (see Matthew 7:1–5).

—Be happy and share your joy and happiness with others. Happy is he who keepeth the law (see Proverbs 29:18).

—Praise, inspire, and encourage others. We need to inspire, urge, and persuade others to be their best. We seek to strengthen and uplift others (see Luke 22:32; Isaiah 35:3).

—Live with hope, and help others grasp on to hope (see Romans 15:4). Hope is in Christ and God the Father (see 1 Timothy 1:1; Jeremiah 17:7).

—Be kind and gentle. Loving-kindness is always right (see Ephesians 4:32; Colossians 3:12).

—Be forgiving. In forgiving, the baggage of sins is cast away (see Luke 6:37).

—Help the poor and needy (see Proverbs 14:21; 28:27). This is pure religion (see James 1:27).

—Be good, and go about doing good. This is the essence of life, for that is what Christ did in all things, from Gethsemane to the cross and the Garden Tomb and throughout His life full of love and goodness: "How God anointed Jesus of Nazareth with the Holy Ghost and with power: who went about doing good, and healing all that were oppressed of the devil; for God was with him" (Acts 10:38).

This is what life is all about: going about doing good—lifting the helpless hands and strengthening the feeble knees—and then the scripture is fulfilled, "Verily I say unto you, Inasmuch as ye have done it unto one of the least of these my brethren, ye have done it unto me" (Matthew 25:40). This is the spirit of Christmas. This is living a Christlike life. This is where true happiness is found, in blessing and serving others.

Now tell us your story by posting it on MrGsLegacyLivesOn.blogspot.com. You will inspire and bless lives forever.

About the Author

Ed J. Pinegar is the author of more than sixty nonfiction books, audio books, and talks. He is passionate about the life and teachings of Jesus Christ, who gives hope to all, and it is Ed's Christmas wish that all may have hope and come to realize the goodness of God. He and his wife are the parents of eight children and the grandparents of thirty-eight grandchildren, and they have twenty-four great-grandchildren. He invites you to participate in the online Blogspot—mrgslegacyliveson.blogspot.com to share your wonderful experiences in following Mr. G's Christmas wish.